Mama Bear
Tell Your
Story

Mama Bear Tell Your Story

Inspired By A True Story

LONDON

MAMA BEAR TELL YOUR STORY
INSPIRED BY A TRUE STORY

iUniverse books may be ordered through booksellers or by contacting:

iUniverse
1663 Liberty Drive
Bloomington, IN 47403
www.iuniverse.com
844-349-9409

ISBN: 978-1-6632-1651-9 (sc)
ISBN: 978-1-6632-1652-6 (e)

Print information available on the last page.

iUniverse rev. date: 01/11/2021

Hi, my name is London

This book is to help young mothers and
women. Young men and older men.
The lost, the misfit`s, the Stand alone
Just to give you a warning this book is or may
not be for the common intellectual.

This book isn`t divided in to chapters, and because of
how the storm of life was so continuously going.

There is life after 8 mile

Innocent (token away) Deception
Deceit

Is nothing but hurt and confusion.

Gambling (little bro)

Watching my brother go through half Million in one summer.

Alcoholism (ma and me) Drugs (ma, ma bro) Coma (me)

Death (serving and dealing) Rape (me)
Sex (young and for $)

Jail or prison (me and my bro) Teenage ma
Men in my life (reuniting what's a teenage Crush and husbands)
Married and Divorce (feeling like the anther women and
having another women playing your identity) Mental
and Physical abuse (your son walking in the room with
a gun in your face. Your kids being abused without your knowledge)

Being a sister and not

Not knowing your Dad (you can live on)

High school Diploma (Doesn't matter how
old your) Graduate from Hair school
Fighting with God.

Army ma

Happy every after

Recognition

I want to thank everybody from my heart the help me get through the end of this book. With Editing of this book and coming together as a community of Friendship, family and as a church.

To my older kids love you guys to the end of now meaning. We have been through a hell of a fight. But what makes me sleep at night if knowing how we fought as a family and never let anything keep us done Worriers we are.

Thank you my family the couple that's still around you mean the world to me finally, I want to thank you to my Church and thank you for not letting me go and being Family and a community. And thank you Lord for putting your roots into me to let me know I am home.

Who Hears
Her Cry

Cookies and cream

Gumdrops lemon ice
vanilla ice cream cones and chocolate bars
baby dolls and strawberry shortcakes

Cotton candy and popcorn and all the kid's rides you can see.

Time to take a walk behind closed doors and it's not a movie.

And sugar and spice isn't always nice

Growing up in my house, I do remember my mother doing what she had to do to make things work to make sure my brother and I had what we needed. It also helped along the way to have some good family and friends to try and help.

People sometimes wonder how far back we could remember. I have a memory of a dark-haired man with a mustache looking down at me, and so I asked my ma about this. Come to find out it, was my dad. She said the last time my dad saw me was when I was about two years old. She told me of how he left us right around Christmas when he was supposed to get food and presents for the house, and never returned. He left her pregnant and with a little son. Come to find out it wasn't the first time he had left her.

She was pregnant with me and he left her in Arizona and my grandparents had to fly her back to Michigan. Grandma told me she should of stuck to her grounds because my mother told her the Carnies are going to marry them on top of the Ferris wheel and they were going to run away with the Carnies. My father was adopted by the people that owned the carnival, there was about 13 kids, some adopted and some blood brothers and sisters.

I know my happy place was at my grandparents house because it was always safe there. I Love my grandfather very much. He was a hard worker who would work two or three jobs to provide a roof over my mom and her siblings head and whatever they needed.

My grandfather was in the Navy and stationed in New York. He was born in Pennsylvania, he had Polio when he was a kid that put him in a wheelchair temporarily. He was a drinker and my mother had memories of Grandma and Grandpa fighting of her getting hit and watching her siblings get hit as well. She was kicked out of the house in the winter time because grandpa was drunk.

My grandmother used to tell me how my mother was kicked out of Catholic School when she was a teenager, after being found drunk in an alley. Grandma got her home to hide her from

Grandpa Come to find out my grandfather's dad was a alcoholic and would beat him and put him down as well.

My mother also quit school two months before she should have graduated from high school. She did go back to school for her GED and got work and a trade and construction.

Grandma did try to make the best of it for everybody. But with grandpa's past upbringing and abuse with his father, it was reflected with their family now. Grandma was born in Poland with a very wholesome family and then moved to the USA. She met my grandfather in New York and got married and stayed for a while in New York because he was stationed in the Navy there. When grandpa was done with the Navy, they moved to Michigan.

I remember my mother as a bartender because it was one of my happy moments as a kid. Getting change from people, playing video games and trying to play pool, but people telling me I was too little. I remember eating French fries, chips and candy. One of my mother's live-in boyfriends, who she thought was on insulin, was really on heroin. He would make me kneel on dried macaroni noodles in a corner if I didn't listen to him and then this monster would hit me. I remember going to the hospital to get the dry noodles removed from my knees. I think back now what could a three-year-old do so wrong to deserve this! I guess you can say it's a little messed up being a kid being afraid in your own home.

I remember sharing a room with my little brother, who was in a crib across from my bed. My bed was up by a window and one day, it closed on my hands. I heard the monster walking, and with tears running down my face, I laid there and I couldn't even scream for help. All of a sudden, I heard a door close. I started to scream for my mother and she finally came and freed up my hands.

The monster had me one day kneeling on the dry noodles, and my ma came home and saw him asleep in the chair with a needle by him. My ma grabbed me from the floor and screamed at him to get out, which he did. I never saw him again, and found out later he had overdosed on heroin.

I remember my brother and I were around my grandparents a lot. My grandma was always trying to teach me something from numbers to the alphabet or speaking Polish, and, always telling me to sit up straight because lit- tle ladies don't slouch. I always loved listening to music and dancing or watching grandma sew costumes for my aunt or putting us down for nap to watch her soaps. We lived down the side street from their house, and when I was little she told me I somehow got out the house and walked down to her house. She heard this little voice and she was sitting on the porch yelling "LONDON, don't cross, I'm coming."

Grandma hid me for a moment from my mother. I heard her crying and my grandma yelling at her and telling her that her drinking and getting high with friends were more important than your own daughter. I came out of hiding and told her to stop crying because I'm here. When we were young, my little brother (don't know how he did it) turned the stove on and my ma woke up to a fire around her bed and her fingers burning. We went to grandma's house and she was so mad at my brother and she made him touch the lighter when it was on, and he ran from her and hid under the table until she stopped. My grandpa always worked a lot, but before he took his nap before his next job, he always brought home these little round cheeses or candies. Grandpa would always take us to church every Sunday.

Going to church I always felt hope. We would go across the street on the corner, there was an ice cream shop and then we would go see the fire trucks across from the ice cream shop. It didn't seem not fair after that my ma's boyfriend Mr. Jerk entered our lives.

It always seemed to start off good with the new boyfriend. Memories of nice family holidays, birthdays, or dinners that would lead to the inevitable fight's and bickering. Something small as walking by the television blocking a touchdown pass would lead to an argument or worse. On my 7 or 8 birthday. This would take place and the fighting was so extreme, they forgot my cake and ice cream. Happy Birthday to me huh..... I'd lived on Mitchell Street on the border of Detroit and Hamtramck. The neighborhood kids and I were always playing and running around like all kids. Our favorite was playing in the flooded streets after a hard rainfall, on a hot summer day.

We played all the typical kid games, but one day a certain game would change things. One morning we'd gone out to play hide and seek, needless to say that day I had in the wrong spot. Tucked between two cars seemed to be the perfect place to hide. I would soon regret that choice. After being found I darted from my spot in surprise, which also surprised an oncoming car. Screeching tires gave way to my face catching the bumper. I didn't re-member much, only my mother holding me while the warm blood gushed from my mouth. Finding out shortly after that I'd almost bit off my tongue. After getting stitched, I'd have a lifelong reminder in the form of a J on my tongue. The family would then have a saying that if I ever went missing, look for the J and they would know it was me. Thankful that never happened. I'd gone to my grandparent's where my brother also lived off and on. My grandparent's felt the need to care for the two of us after the accident. One morning I heard a knock at the door, my bedroom was at the front of the house by the porch. I opened the window to see a lady asking "are you the girl I hit?" I said yes and she immediately started to tell me how sorry she was and how God was with me. She had come with gifts, game, candy, and a fully piggy bank. That would be the only and last time I would ever see her. I'd always felt safe with my grandparents and never wanted to leave. Although they too would have moment of bickering and fighting, they loved each other. My grandma would chase grandpa around with a frying pan at times, spewing a few choice words in Polish at him in which he didn't understand half the time. We would learn later in life that the words weren't nice at all. I remember my grandma and Aunt Ja Ja would always sew the most beautiful dresses for their traveling polish dance group. They went all over to different states and cities, and even outside the country at times. She even made mine for Polish Pride Festival in Hamtramck. I would walk with my aunt in the parade and have a ball.

My mother was the type of person that would not let us go hungry or without anything we needed. Although on Welfare, she'd found different places for help such as Focus Hope or area churches. Even resorting to the occasional theft from a grocery store to put food on the table. One time she had gotten caught and I was with her. At the jail, I can recall an officer sitting at his desk. To ease my stress, he'd given me a large candy cane. He told me that my grandparents were coming for me. I began to cry when asking about my mother. He then took me to see her in the holding cell. She hugged and kissed me, then said that all will be fine when they arrive to get me. Walking back from the cell to the police officer desk he said "now that's where the bad people stay". I told him "my Ma wasn't a bad person" When finely released she had come for my brother and I to return home with her.

But to our surprise there was a man neither of us had known or seen before. It was another boyfriend! Jerk that-my mother had moved into our house. At first he seemed very nice, as they all do. But that would soon change as well. For reasons unknown, we were always getting smacked around, yelled at, or tending to his needs like we were servants. Hell. The dog got better treatment than we did. We couldn't even sit on the couch, but the dog could. Because my ma always worked odd hours, she would leave us with jerk. I recall one night at the dinner table I had got sick and threw up in my plate. He made me stay at the table and tried to force me to eat the spoiled meal as he smaked the back of my head. I couldn't leave the table, I fell asleep and was their until my mom picked me up from the chair when she got home late from work. She cleaned me up then placed me in bed. The next morning, the plate was still on the table with the half eaten, regurgitated food still on it.(I hear him" I should make me eat that!!".) Then out of what seemed like thin air, my mother appears to discard the plate. The two of them argued, but she still allowed him to stay.

I love it when my grandfather would come get us for church. After service he would always take us for ice cream across the street from church. The best was having all the family together for my communion. And construction with NO fighting or arguments. And the fond memories of the pretty dress I'd worn that day.

Start to grow up

When the family got together, Phil never acted the same like he did when he was behind closed doors. But my grandma did say she didn't like how he always Aren't in front of us or would always ask my brother or I to get him things, but she knew not to say anything, because my mother would of kept me and brother from her. As I and my brother started to get older, he started to get meaner but never in front of people. My mother started to stop working at bars, and got a job at the Hazel Park race track. I had fun going there with my ma, but she would get mad in a funny way because she would get done picking her numbers or horses out, and as we were watching the races, I would call the horse's number out and they would win. So my mother tried to get me to pick them before she would play them and they wouldn't come out, until one sat there and watched and I called them and they did. Let's just say she was happy.

When I was in the fifth grade I started being the big kid in my class. When my mother would go work at night at the race track, we would take our baths before we would go to bed. He always told my brother to take his bath first. As I would start to finish my bath and get out to dry myself off, he would always come in to rub lotion on me and touch places he shouldn't be touching. After the first time, I think my body went into shock because I got so numb and a cold and frozen feeling ran through me. I didn't know what to do. After he would get done, he would always tell me not to say anything to anyone and would always threaten me by saying he would hurt my mother or my grandparents, and saying I wouldn't see them anymore. Well he started beating on my mother to the point, that he kicked her so hard, I got out my bed yelling at him to stop because my mother was on the floor and not moving. He smacked me and told me to get back to my room. I hid in my room till my grandparents came and got me and my little brother. Come to find out, she had to have her spleen removed because he kicked her so hard. Finely she came and got me and my brother, but he was still there.

Things started being happy for a moment. By sixth grade, I started looking like a sixteen year old. He started coming in my room. He put his hand around my throat and continued on raping me. It happened a few times. By the time I was thirteen, I started a job at a neighborhood store. I started middle school and I tried to stay away from home so I started to join sports. I loved basketball and was getting really good at it. I didn't like getting paid at times because he would take some of my money, so I ended up quitting because of it. I guess my ma paying the bills and the state wasn't enough for him. My friends and I would hang out at the pizza place on Jos. Compau in Hamtramck. There were these older guys that would always try and talk to us. On our way to the school, we would stop to go to play a basketball game. There was a car with a couple of guys that I would see driving around where we hung out, that followed us to the school. They kept telling us to come with them, but we told them no. Walking up to the school, I had my back to them and one of the guys jumped out of their car and grabbed me from behind, trying to put me in the back seat! I kept kicking in the door yelling at him to stop! He didn't stop until my principal came out and then they dropped me there and took off. I went to play basketball the next morning in school and got called down to the office. There were police there and ended up taking that guy to court. He got charged for attempted kidnapping and got sent back to his country. Let me tell you, my mother and didn't think we were going to make it out of there alive because the room was full of his family!

Not too long after, Phil was up to his old ways again, by coming into the bathroom and in my bedroom. It was summer time and I ran away. My ma's friend C, which she grew up with, took me down to Cass Corridor to show me she working women hanging off the porches. I came back home and things stopped for a while. As it started up again with Phil, it was the day before Thanksgiving and I ran away. My best friend at the time was trying to talk me out of running away, but I didn't listen to her. I found an abandoned garage with a broken-down car in it. She didn't want to leave me alone and I kept telling her to go home, but she didn't. We stayed overnight in the cold with nothing to eat, so we started to eat snow because we had nothing to drink. The next day was Thanks- giving and she kept asking me to go with her, but I didn't. When she left, I just remembered wanting to die, and I even found some broken glass to try to cut myself. My friend must have told somebody I was there because the cops came and got me and took me to the hospital. After I got back home, Phil tried coming in my room again to rape me. I remember going to my grandparent's house and I think they went shopping, but my Aunt C was watching us and she went to lay down. My grandparents and my Aunt C has a lot of different medications inside the house. I started off in my grandma's room by taking some pills, and then took some from my grandfather and then finally took some pills from my aunt. I thought I took them all, but I didn't know I dropped some of them and my little brother took them too. My ma and grandparents made it home in time, and I remember going to the hospital with a tube down my throat and throwing up black stuff. After the doctors got me stable, my ma yelled and me and asked me "why do you keep doing these crazy things?" I didn't know my little brother was fighting for his life, and she pulled the curtain and looked at him with tubes coming out of his mouth and lines on his chest. She yelled at me and said it would be all my fault if he dies. All I wanted was her arms around me, but instead I was back in my cold place. Well everything seem to calm down for a moment again Not to fair after Christmas was coming. My brother had got a pair of boxing gloves and all he wanted to do was learn how to defend his self, he was about nine or ten.

Phil told him to put him gloves on and he did. As I'm watching so you want to fight he started to hit him like he was a man. He was hitting so hard my brother was bouncing on the wall crying for him to stop and he started to bleed. I started to yell at him and he look at me and said do you want this to. I said to him you can't be a Dad and show him how to defend his self against the kids that made fun of him because he was in special education and had a speech problem because my mom was drinking alcohol when she was pregnant with him. Then he said; are you scared to put on the gloves yourself. I don't know what came over me, but I told him I don't need the gloves.

He told me he would leave them on so he wouldn't hurt me. I told him pain only hurts for a second right. He would always hurt us no matter what we tried to play or do or always telling us to suck up. He hit me a couple of times really good that I see stars. I had got so mad and took with what all I had and run into him hard we fell in between the table and coach. I would not stop hitting him until I heard my little brother," London please stop," and I see blood on my hands. Next thing I know my brother and I are sitting in front of the TV eating cereal and my ma walks in and Jerk was sitting with a ice pack on his eye and she ask him what happen he said ask your daughter. I told her pain only hurt for a second right ma and I'm looking at him saying.

Brother and Sister Love

There is one other time me and my brother and some neighborhood kids were playing touch football and Mr. Jerk comes out wanting to play in the street tackle football. While we were playing it was getting very aggressive game. My brother and the neighborhood friends kept going for the grass and falling on it. I started to face him and started to get mad because he couldn't get a hold of me to tackle me. I started to walk away and next thing I know he hit me in the back of the head with the football. I turned around and said ok lets play. We went into form to play I went after him hit into him so hard we both fall and he went shoulder first into the curb.

Well needless to say someone needed surgery. After he healed up he got a really good job at factory job and he left my mother for someone that work there. Sad as I watched her try and kill herself over him. After he was gone ma started drinking more and hanging out in the bars, I don't know what happened, but my ma went back to school for her GED with a license in construction trade.

For a while it seem things were going good, she went to work and still hung out at bars. One night she was raped by a gang. My Uncle Dee got her and took care of her, at the house she didn't want no cops or the hospital. She wasn't herself for a while, start to drink a lot more. Always down on herself and always crying. Me and my brother start hanging out on the streets. I started hanging out with more older people and started to do adult things and went shopping a lot. My ma moved us out of Hamtramck for a moment, We move to a trail park in Warren. She started a good job. My brother and I went to school and a couple people weren't very nice to kids that lived in a trail park. You were better known as trash living in a trail park until I show them what trash can do. I would always try and make sure the house was clean and dishes were done and my brother was doing his work. Always had to get him out from under the trail, or he would get a hold of my ma's pot and smoke it under the trailer. I never told on him I always took the palm. She met this one guy he was a truck driver. She would only see him on the weekends. Had nice holidays, always made sure my brother and I were taken care of. He wanted to marry my ma but she didn't, so we started not seeing him around. I tried always to keep myself busy with school and my brother. Well one day my mom met this biker that lived in the house a block over. Sometimes we didn't see her until the next morning or day.

I would get me and my brother ready for school. One day at school I was asked to came to a party by a well know football player at school. That night I told my brother just to stay in the trailer and I would be home soon. When I got there was drinking going on. Things seem to be going cool for a minute. But then everybody was out in the yard and playing around and they had a pool and the football players started to throw people in the pool I was one of them. It started getting late. I ask the football player that asked me to the party to drive me home and he said he would. When we were driving and he went a different way from my house. He stop behind a building and told me he want sex or I could walk home. I didn't have a clue were I was at so I had no other choice in the matter at two a.m. When I finely got home, I just remember crying myself to sleep. My little brother came into my room asking me if I was all right? He gave me a hug and kiss and I then told him he had to go back to bed and I love him. Well on Monday when I had got back to school was getting funny looks from the team and classmates. At lunch I was known as the trail park trash and all the football players asking me if they could have try they can drive me home. I look at the one that took me home and said you known I didn't want to do that you didn't want to take me home. Him and the players said no one would believe me and go about myself trail trash. When I was walking away a teacher ask me what that was about and frozen, I didn't say anything and walked away. Our first year starting off here wasn't very good. I started to be a outcast. Started to hang out with kids that like to drink, smoke and do there dots on paper and not good before gym. Summer time finely came. My ma was still dating the biker on the next block. We always had Bar Q's and a lot of people over love going on motorcycle rides. One day there was this guy next door to my ma's boyfriend, His brother We went to school together we were good friends, he was the only one that I had told about the football party and he said he would never would go to one he wish he knew was going and I should of said some- thing he did not like football players.

Not too far after, I started to clean everything top to bottom. My dog would not leave my side, even stayed by my belly. I had to call my ma from the bar to get home, and it was getting later in the night and there was a black- out, not good. I prayed really hard to get there alive, and I did. I finally arrived at the hospital and was in one big room with three other women. I was trying to keep focused, even though I'm hearing these other women screaming and I am not trying to freak out. I started to think about the birthing class and movies I had watched and the books I read. There was more pain coming, and no baby yet! The nurse would not give me anything for pain, so my mother gave me Tylenol three with codeine. Ma told me not to tell anyone she gave it to me. She was just trying to help.

Finally my son came, Anthony was born on March 31, 1991. My saint my savior, my soul. I remember him on my chest, with my lips on his head and telling him, "I'm going to die trying to keep you safe." Once I got him home, I think my ma couldn't deal with the fact of me being a teenage ma. My grandparents were there setting up the crib for him. I never went anywhere without him. If I went to take a bath, he went with me. He even took baths with me until he pooped in the tub!

My ma started to go to the bars a lot, and she met husband, "Jerk number three." They were bad drunks together, to the point they didn't remember coming home with each other. Even my brother and I started to agree with them and fight. Till one fight

Time to Fight back and Being a Teen age Ma

Welcome to the jungle

Sweet sixteen

It was winter time and I was getting tired of the fighting, especially around my son. I was on my ma's state case with my son, but it was to the point that I didn't care anymore. They came home from the bar almost at closing time, and we all were fighting. People from the neighborhood kept calling and coming over because it started to get really bad even to the point where we were putting hands on each other. I got my son's snow suit on him because I had called my friend a couple blocks away and had to walk in the cold and snow with my son since no one could or would drive us. When I went to put my coat on and pick up my son, my ma and her drunk husband jumped on me with my son in my arms. I fell back in the rocking chair with him and they were on top of us, with me trying to fight with one hand. I looked down at my son, and there was a mark on his forehead from my ma's husband ring. Somehow I pushed them off of me with my brother's help and ran out the door. As I got to the side of the house to leave, from the front of the house, my ma's husband came through the window. He got up and started to fight with me, but some friends outside started to jump over the fence to get at him. The love of having neighborhood family. Went to my friend's house that night and slept on floor with blankets and pillows, but we were warm. We were able to stay a couple of nights but now I didn't know what was next.

Started to stay at different places and some places shouldn't off been with him. Started to sell crack off of Wood- ward out of a building behind closed doors out of a window or a small hole in the door. Started to hang out in Highland Park and always was around the high rollers from the streets. But I stayed away from the ones that came out of jail. I even started hanging out at motorcycle clubs. Always had somewhere to stay, but knew this shouldn't be a life for my son.

My grandfather found me and told me to please comeback home with him and he would help me find my own place. He found me a place next door to him and took me down to DHF to get my own case with my son. This seemed pretty good for a while. I even started to talk to my ma again after the fight we had gotten into al- most year ago. I even had a boyfriend that went bad one day. He fought with me and I was already starting to go through this at 16. Well one day he did it again, hit me and took my rent money. I tried not to get my grandfather involved, and called my friends, but they were out of town, and sent one of their friends called "Pineapple".

He came over in a tuxedo and let the guy know that I was dating, he only had a few minutes to grab what he could and get out. In the meantime my grandfather came over with his shot gun. Pineapple was in the doorway and was talking to my grandpa and opened up his jacket, and grandpa walked away and let him handle it. This went easy and quick. My mother came over to my grandparents' house. We finally started to talk again. She was still with her piece of crap husband, but the place upstairs from her was for rent. Ma asked about me moving there and I did. Her husband and she were always fighting and getting drunk coming home, and here we go again. When I moved upstairs, I started to see my brother hang out with our neighborhood family and there were hanging out with the street gangs. I kept telling him to please stay out of trouble. Started doing my own thing. Hanging out with my girls at Belle Isle. Cars and motorcycles parked and everybody hanging out, either talking crap, or trying to pick you up for the night. I would check on my ma at the corner bar on Caniff. There would be times during the day when I would just hang out or just go to see my ma. She loved her bikers, which I couldn't really understand

That summer he had got a tracker jeep. The one time I did not go for a ride with him, his jeep was known to flip when u turned to fast. One day he did and it flipped and he died. Well me and his older brother started talking and we had got together and started seeing each other. I just turn fifteen he was over twenty. Well that summer I had gotten pregnant with my first son LA. At the end of the summer I'm pregnant and lost a good friend. And now my ma and her biker boyfriend are fighting a lot. My first unborn son father stay by me for a while. One night me and him decided to go back to the trail I so I can lay down because my ma and her boyfriend were fighting. Couple hours later I had got woken up with my ma slamming door and locking it and putting a chair by the door. She had blood on her face and telling us not to answer the door if he comes. Few minutes later here he comes. He is running around the trail yelling bitch you think you are going to leave me and not marry me?

He kept trying to open the door and the back door. He said ok I got something for you it was quiet for a few. My unborn son's father kept getting up looking through the widows to try and see him. We were laying on the pull out bed in the living room. He came back telling my ma I will give you another chance to open the door to let him in. We had a bay window in front of the bed my unborn father yelled at me to get out of the bed, he came in front of that widow and through a cocktail bomb as I was getting off the bed. I got my brother out of his room and we all went to the back door and we could open it, the trailer was so smoking and all you could see was the fire coming and him yelling out enjoy. I started scramming for someone to help us. I couldn't get the door open and a person next door let us out in time he said the door was blocked by the wood. My unborn son's dad went back into the burning trailer to get our dog but couldn't get the cat out. Later he ended up going to jail he was setting on his porch drinking when the cops got him, that as what was told to us by the police. Me and him ended up staying by my aunt's house for a while. I even tried to go back to school in Oak Park and didn't go over very well, some of the girl didn't care for I was to white and I couldn't take a chance on losing my baby. No house, dropped out of school at fifteen and pregnant. Then me and his dad started fighting to the point my aunt and uncle had to get between us. I wish I could remember what the fight was about. My aunt was trying to help and wanted to adopt my son out couldn't do it. She was scared for my future. My ma came and got me so we stayed at her girlfriend's house for a minute. Her eighteen year old daughter was pregnant. Some of my ma others friends were trying to talk me into getting abortion because I'm to young to be having a baby.

The girl that was eighteen and pregnant was showing me pictures of abortion and they were in the garbage bag to. There was no way in hell. Well my ma found an efficiency apartment my Brother, Ma and I stayed there. When she went to work the ladies' at the front desk offered me a job cleaning out the apartment's to help me get money to buy baby stuff. Ma started drinking more again. We went late one day to a store. I was hungry, she stay in the car when I went because she was drunk. By the time I came out of the store she was pass out. The widow was cracked open, finely got her up and got her out and put her in the back seat. I had to learn how to drive not knowing how to at first and I had to drive by a police station at two a.m. Somehow I made it back. We had got enough money up to move back to Hamtramck at a house we lived in three times. Well I had the basic for him and my ma end up putting together a baby shower for me and I had another friends that had baby stuff for me as well. I didn't have a crib just a play pin. My grandparents were a lot of help and couldn't wait for him to get here. Grandma witch it was his great grandma help me pick his name out.

Went to the hospital everything checked out good. On November 19, my grandparents and I went and took the boys to go see Santa and do a little window shopping. I was holding James and my grandpa had Anthony and I started to feel a little funny, so I put him in the stroller. I thought I had peed a little bit on myself, so we went back to their house and I called my ma and the Doctor. I couldn't wait for my ma, so grandpa took me to the hospital and waited to see what the doctor had to say. My water broke and they had to start my contractions. As I turned my head to say something to my grandfather, he was gone. (LOL) I talked to my ma on the phone and she asked if I was ok because she couldn't make it there and I told her, "We got this". Early morning on November 20, 1994, Jacqualine- Jane Claire was here. They put her on my chest and I kissed her head and told her, saying I'm going to be best ma I could be or would die trying to keep her safe. Well her dad came and got me from the hospital and took us to the house where her brothers were waiting for us.

For a while, it was good seeing their dad so happy because he had a little girl and his sons. He even got a real job.

Street life or your family. We even got his ma to come to grandma's house for Thanksgiving. Baby Jackie was a week old that first Thanksgiving with grandmas and great grandparents, aunts and uncles. It was going good for a minute. My aunt didn't care much for Jackie's dad because of the fighting, but she was drinking and called him out. Grandpa snatched her up and pushed her in the bathroom locking her in it. My ma and grandfather and other family kept apologizing for her mouth and asked them to stay awhile longer. Peanut and Mama Clair stayed for a while. One time I did go to his grandma's house for the holidays. I love food, but for one thing was a little scared about the chitlins. Tried them with some hot sauce and then they were ok. On our way home from Highland, we were shot at! Thank God no one was hurt. Well after the New Year, things started to get crazy again. He started to not be very helpful anymore with money, and started going out or not coming home till the next day. Started to ask my grandparents for money. The last fight we had was over all his cheating on me. I had a chance to move back to my ma's. The house that she was renting from had the downstairs available to rent. I moved in with my three kids and Peanut went our separate ways. One night I went into my kid's room that they shared; Jackie in a crib, James in a play pen and Anthony on a single mattress on the floor. I started to feel sick to my stomach. I knew that I my kids deserved better than this, so I started to think about what I could do. Here I was, nineteen years old, with three kids, no diploma and no money. Their dad did try to come back, but there was already a lot of hurt involved and I wanted better life for my kids and me because I found out later she was raped by a gang of bikers, but had a club that always looked out for her. One day my friend met a guy and his cousin at Belle Isle from Highland Park. She was trying to talk to this guy named "Peanut" and his cousin tried to talk to me, but that didn't happen! But one day he realized how much she was a hoe. I learned from what I have seen of Peanut that you don't mess with him. Well we started talking, and next thing I knew, we were about to have a little peanut on the way. My brother was hanging out one day skipping school with his friend and they were at a friend's house listening to loud music and playing around with guns. Well boys will be boys, and my brother saw a friend of his falling to the ground and ran to him and asked him if he was ok. His friend looked at him, and asked him the same thing because it wasn't his friend that got shot. My brother had gotten shot through his arm! Found out later it went through his arm centimeters from his heart. He was shot with a twelve gauge saw-offed shotgun. Before they got to the house, my aunt was calling my ma asking where my brother was at. Not very long after, his boys pulled up screaming that they had taken my brother to the hospital. I opened up the back door of the car and sat inside. After I closed the door, I started to look around and saw blood was everywhere, even on my hand. I started to pray so hard for my brother to be alive when I got to the Hospital. When I got there, my ma wasn't there yet, so the doctors were asking me to give them permission to get him airlifted down town because he was in bad shape. I remember seeing him before they left for a couple of seconds and held his hand and told him "please don't die on me", and his eyes closed as they took him. I went outside the hospital and his friends were there.

Thank God I remembered I was pregnant with my second son, but told them my brother better not die because they will join him! My baby brother did live. My Ma and Grandparents did sue the parent of the house that he was shot in. By the time what needed to be paid out, he had close to $500,000. My grandparents put it in a trust where he until he was at least twenty one. My brother had a long recovery to go. Aside from the recovery, my brother was mentally challenged and had a speech problem. We had to go back and forth to the hospital a lot because pieces from the gun shot had to be removed. As he was getting better, my son Anthony and Peanut moved, and then we little peanut, James Derek, born October 5, 1993. 1993 was the year I should have graduated from High School, but when I held him and put him on my chest it felt like he stole my heart. A few months later, found out we had a little girl on the way. We started fighting more and nothing like learning how to throw cans of veggies at each other! We moved from Davison, which wasn't too safe at times since you had to teach your kid to stay on the floor from shootings that were happening nearby! We ended up moving to Hamtramck. Before our daughter was born we had gotten into a really big fight and he gave me a black eye. As I was leaving the house to get away from him, I fell down the stairs. He wouldn't take me to the hospital, so I waited for him to leave and called my grandfather to take me to the hospital to make sure my baby was ok. I made sure to cover up my black eye before my grandfather came.

Boy Did I Find A Job

We rented the house from the guy that was helping the owner with fixing the house up and get the rent. He was also the agent for the gentlemen's clubs. The first one I ever walked into was downtown called "The Grind". I had to walk up three floors to get to the dressing room and it had no door to it, and outside the room was the pool table. Not a cool feeling. It was my first time in heels and I had to walk back three floors down and then get on stage, and a little stage at that. I couldn't wait to get off stage and get dressed. We made one more stop on Michigan Ave. Southwest. It was during the day when we were going to the next gentlemen's club. We saw women walking around and some of these women needed real help because they couldn't stay awake! Some of the women couldn't understand why they were on the streets because they were beautiful, but I guess that's what drugs do to you. There were a lot of different bars on the avenue, but we ended up at a place called My Bar Two. It was a truck driver stop and at one point, a ma and daughter owned it and they were changing it into a gentlemen's club. The DJ, "M" asked me what my stage name was going to be. I had no clue, so he told me to look at my name because it was right there! London. Three women in the dressing room D, C and S were trying to make me laugh because they saw how nervous I was and said, "come on Darling, you have to pick a name." So "London" was born.

Before I went on stage he asked me about music and I couldn't think of a single song. I see why dancers hold a pole so much or run back and forth; either they can't dance, nerves or can't walk in those high-heels. Well I did my three stage song and didn't care for the third stage because it was where a beer tap should have been, and it shouldn't have been a stage with only four feet to work with. Well, to get on it, I fell into the lower bar thinking it was the way to get on it. They still hired me and I didn't start till the next night. I called a cab to go to work on the avenue. There were cops are all over the place. Found out they found a dead dancer in the garbage bin outside the back of the bar. But off to work I went. Things seemed a little more crazy at night. Girls you would walk past, look at you funny or would tell you not to sit there because they were sitting there. I was trying to watch the other girls dance to see what they were doing before I did my first dance. Some were even fighting with guys because they wouldn't keep their hands to themselves, Mr. M was always watching over the girls. I did ask him about trying a day shift just to see where I wanted to be and he said it wouldn't be a problem. I finished out the night because not only was I getting paid by check for $11 or $12 an hour, but I always had my tips from stage and dances. When I went to get dressed I saw this board up by the bathroom and M came in and marked a line by someone's name. I asked him about it and he said it is a game they play with the dancers about who makes a guy run out after doing a dance. I'm asked why would a guy just want to run out of here and he said, wouldn't you after you came in your pants! Well the next day I tried the day shift, and it seemed to work. D, C, and S were being very helpful and I always watched them because they had all had different ways about them. Loved D with her outfits and loved her in hats and then C had confidence and bad ass attitude and lastly S the gracefulness of her dancing and pole work on stage. All three showed me how to

LONDON

do a good dance. Well let's put it this way; I guess my dance was good because I made the board in the dressing room. The dances were ten dollars each in a chair back by the walk. The second guy I danced for paid for ten dances in a row and that was a lot of work! The next day that I came into work D told me she wanted me to meet this guy that comes in every now then, and you'll make about a hundred dollars, sometime a little more. He likes to order a lot of gassy foods. So if she sees me, wave me over to come sit. I see her wave me over and I went over and sat down and told him my name and he asked me "what was I into?" I came back and told him, my kids and dancing. But he asked me again, "do I have any fetishes?" I asked him what did that mean? In the meantime here comes some food - chili, chili fries, burrito's and some other stuff to make you gassy. So the customer started to talk again, and told me his fetish is to watch women eat and then dance for him and fart in his face! I got up and left. What the hell is wrong with this guy! Even though I was starting to see things and hear things I never heard before, I was making $300 to $500 a night cash starting and had a paid check, and things were starting to look up. There was a day I was at work and this women walked in. The girls told me to watch her because when she gets drunk, she tries to rape the new girls. Well I was on one of the stages and sure as hell, she grabbed my leg, saying she wants to eat me. Trying to get her off me took three other people to help me get her off my leg! The next time, she came in M had a talk with her, and she came up to me to apologize. After work one day, I wanted to check out a couple other bars on the avenue so I went into the Brass Key Bar. They had stand-up showers there where bar guys would have to pay to go in the dances and play with glow soap and wash yourself with g` string on. It was fun, but never did it again. I even checked out Maricons. But stuck it out for a while at the My Bar Two. I even got my one girl friend to try it out where

I was working. She liked the money because it was easy to make once you got over strange men touching you and putting up with drunk men, but you did have the ones that were easy going. I was asked if I would meet outside the bar for more money, and I passed on that. One day my friend asked me would I ever think about being with a women? I told her I never thought about it because of that girl attacking me on stage and we laughed. She wanted me to think about doing it with her because she didn't want to try it with someone she didn't know.

We did get together at the hotel and I don't think we really knew what we were doing, but it did end our friendship after that.

When I first started dancing, I was only smoking weed. People were offering me cocaine, ecstasy, Adderall, zany bars and pain pills. Girls even had their own alcohol in their bags. My friend and I would smoke weed before we would go into work and you would see some of the dancers drinking as well in their cars before work. One thing you can say was this job wasn't for anyone sober, unless you were on probation or they had a tether or even alcohol tether where they couldn't? In my first year, I watched a girl overdose.

My twenty first birthday at My Bar Two started off by having fun with my manager Mike at midnight the day before my birthday by having a shot of hennessy. Let's just say I'm glad I didn't wake up with a hangover. One day this guy walks in and gives me more attention than normal. All of a sudden, I would see him in the bar a lot more. Mr. Pedophile (at the time I didn't know he really was) started to take me out on dates and showing me a different life style from what I was used to. Took me to nice places to eat and bought my kids and me nice things. I was also dating other people at the time. One day he was at my work waiting for me and saw I was with some- one else. He started to say he wanted to be the only one and how much he loved me and the kids. He said that he was here and their fathers were not, and not too many men would want to love someone else's kids like he was. He asked me, haven't I showed you a better way of living. From there, we started to have a relationship and he asked me to look for another bar. So I asked my agent at the time about looking for another bar to work at.

I went to Seven Mile off of Van Dyke at a place called the Please Station. It was a little hole-in-the-wall bar, but it didn't matter. Met a couple of cops that would come in there. Well the neighborhood was kind of crazy. One day my mother was fighting with my brother because he wanted to get his money because he found out he could get it out when he was eighteen. Well they went back and forth for a minute and finally my mother and grandparents broke down and gave it to him. My brother didn't even care he would have to pay a big fine to take it out early.

My brother started to buy all kinds of things, even had friends and girls as well that wanted to be around, He was even a high tipper at the one club as was working at, the girls that worked their told me my brother was a hundred dollar tipper on stage. He would also love going to this message places and they did have happy endings. He help me a little bit with getting my future in layaway out but wouldn't even help are ma with anything. One day I called my brother why I was at work but he said he was around hanging out with his friends that he couldn't come get me. Well I ended up working a double that night. When I got home at two a.m., my brother came running through the door telling me and our ma that if anyone comes to the door he was here all night with the family. Kept asking him what the hell is going on and all he could say is just please do what I ask and then he went upstairs to sleep.

Well the next morning my eyes weren't really open, went for the door answer it and a cop help push my door open and pushed his way in, asking were my brother was at because the cops new us. They went through my house to the back door to get up stairs, my brother didn't even open up his yet but had hand cuffs on him. My ma asks the cops to please let him put his cloths on and not take him out in his under wear and they did.

Well when we finely found out what had happen my brother drove his so called friends over to a house bored of Detroit and Hamtramck. Why he waited in the car he friends went into this house, they robbed and shot and killed the guy. When they came out the house and running to my brother's car, they had guns on them. Telling him to take off. When we were visiting him why he was waiting to be sentenced to Accessory to murder. One of the anther guys were running their month that went inside the house but was saying my brother was when he wasn't. Watching my ma going through watching her son locked up wasn't a beauty sight at all. One day when we went downtown Detroit to visit him. I was so mad and wanted to get sick to my stomach it was in my throat and I couldn't see straight. They had tide my brother to the bed and covered his face beating him. His teeth were half broken and his face was so beaten almost didn't know who he was. He even had broken ribs. I knew one of the guards their later that night he came up to my job and told me when he went into the cell he found a sock with bars of soap in that what they beat him with. One day we also got a phone call that my brother tried hanging himself but they got him in time and it smells. They had moved him to I guess you want to call the psych ward the jail diagnosed him bipolar schizophrenic manic depressant bipolar. On top of it of him being slow my mom drinking with them she was pregnant he already had that she's growing up it's not even to something deeper. They finally placed my brother and Ionia Michigan from downtown Detroit. One of the guys that were in the house when they shot a guy was putting the blame on my brother was talking about them but my brother really didn't even speak to them because of what they were putting him through but he was never unloyalty to them. When my brother got to his placement I guess they try to mess with him one more time come to find out I guess it's good to know a lot of people especially from the streets, new me that was in there. Let's put it this way the next 5 years wouldn't be hard for him anymore. I always make sure my mother got to talk to him because he was far away for us to get to him paying five hundred dollar phone bills a month making sure he had a bank account with three hundred a month, clothing, anything he needed and also helping out people that were looking out for him as well. Hell I think I even bought a TV forever floor he was moved on to because that's the only thing they wouldn't let him move so where floor they put him on in prison. I wasn't able to see him very much I was working at the gentlemen's club a lot. Paying my bills taking care of my mother and my brother when he was in prison.

When A Pedophile has you Fooled

I was working at My Bar Two there is this man he was a mechanic he kept coming in there after work wanting to get to know and kept asking me for a date. One day I finely broke down. Our first date he took me to the revolving room. Was very nice. He started buying me nice things and the kids too. He's very caring always playing with the kids. Showing love I'm feeling I've never seen before or what you seen on TV. I don't know what it was but I started to pull away from him but he was never letting that happen he was always persistent that we stayed together that there is no other man like him that would be with a woman with children and take care of them or show them any fatherly love like he well. The man throw in my face where is their father not here being one being one.

He also started to show me how to save money because I was making a decent amount not to be. Nice dinners vacations cruises. I even finally learned how to drive at twenty one he got me a Mustang it was an older one but it was mine and it was a convertible and it was my favorite car. We moved in together finally on the Westside. We were starting to buy nice things the kids had go-karts bikes a lot of nice things. But come to find out the neighborhood was not too nice. When you start riding around with your forty five in your front seat driving around asking people did they see anybody around in a go kart you know it's time to move when you are changing them down. They lived in a three-bedroom flat. In the mix to my last my grandfather was diagnosed with prostate cancer felt like I lost a big part of me when he died. My grandmother was sending out by herself alone very often so I ended up moving her in besides my three kids and we ended up moving in his son as well they were all in one room when grandmother was in one can my brother would sleep on the couch in the living room.

We ended up selling her house and we had a savings for me working as a dancer. When Grandma said the house the money was split up fairly between her children and me for taking care of her and moving her in. My uncle came from Florida kept telling everybody going to be at the house so grandma can you give them there share. Well I didn't know until after he left he just didn't leave with his share of the money. I haven't seen him but maybe one time after that he got into a drunk driving accident perming somebody but when they caught up with them he's already too sick from drinking he died cirrhosis of the liver a night alone in Florida in the hospital because I didn't have a chance to get to him and my aunt and cousin. The day he died we're getting ready to get on a plane got a phone call that he was gone. Sad to say his body was left in Florida. But we took our share of the money and bought four level home Downriver Something I never seen before or even walk into to, It was like in a movie.

Back up the kids and grandma and husband about to be. He was showing me and the kids a good life, instead of leaving a life on welfare. Slumlords and the added pets to your home cockroaches and rats. We had a motor- cycle, boat, and a house with a Jacuzzi and a gazebo outside the kitchen. I bought my first car off of a showroom flooring brand new Lincoln LS chase.

Being the girl from the streets at 22, 23 living the Fairytale life of American Dream. And let him have controlling the money I was making about a 100 to a 130,000a year, he was a mechanic at a local shop. Making about 30 to 40,000 a year and also had insurance for everybody.

Not too far after we moved in there I all of sudden was at work 7 days a week. I didn't even get to enjoy the condo that we bought in Florida that made me one time because I was always at work. Wasn't bad bringing home about five thousand a week sometimes that was ass all week. But it led into heavy drinking $100 in cocaine a day and a memory not realizing or knowing what the hell is going on around me. One your on April Fool's Day just from being overly drinking drugging and always overworked I'm starting to be a nice person get into it with somebody at the barn that night I was working at centerfolds I left the bar very upset go to my truck had no business even driving. Got in my truck to go down river we bought our house didn't make it home as I was driving onto go over the bridge trying to do a line at the same time I was hit from the back and the front light in different cars in the third lane bouncing off the wall rolling my truck sliding down the bridge in an instant Screaming God please no it's Sparks and Fire Starting. I remember once the truck stopped trying to find a way out because I was throwing to- wards the back of my blazer seen an area opening proceeded to crawl out of it not realizing at the same time every because when I flipped the truck three times it smashed it down the driver side the only thing you could see was a steering wheel thank God I didn't have my seatbelt on. Scalping my own head from a piece of glass sticking out but kept pushing myself out of the area to get out. Until I stood up looking around hearing people, are you all right and asking me who flew over the bridge but you come to find out it was my bag from work. I turn to look at everybody standing quietly looking at me all of a sudden

I felt something wet on my face they took my hand to wipe it and it was blood my Scout proceeded to slide off of my head and hit me on the side of my face I felt the top of my head screaming can somebody help me next thing I know I'm in a fireman's arms screaming at me please don't fall asleep you can't die on me. Next thing I know I'm in an ambulance downtown Atlanta Hospital fighting with doctors telling me to calm down I got hat one plant a dad cuz I had to do a blood transfusion I started blacking out. I woke back up for a minute with a cop next to me trying to get me to do a breathalyzer which I did a couple of them blowing a 4.0 the doctor proceeded to come in telling me in front of the police officer my cocaine Level could have killed for horses. Next thing I know I'm waking up opening up my eyes to a white light then seeing my family all around me I was in a neck brace. Everybody thanking god because I just came out of a coma. I remember my grandma holding my hand tell me the Lord had his hand on me, I started to laugh and told her yes did he slammed me all over the freeway to wake my ass up. The doctor came in and my ma told him that I was fine why everybody was laughing. The Doctor came in and looking me over and telling me that he didn't mean for me to take him so seriously when he came back into the room where I was at telling me about my Coke level could have killed for horses and I went right into my coma after. I looked at him I said wouldn't you when you have a police officer next to you had to get out somehow. He just looked at me and smiled and said you're going to be fine God is with you. I did tell my grandma later I was with grandpa and he push me to go back that I had to. April fools day was the Acta dent April 12 I was back to work with stiches and staples in my head but tiring to waitress. My husband #1 basically force me back to work tiring to say we had no money but had to go to court because of the crash I was in. My son James when I was home said I look like I didn't know who he and his brothers and sister were. And he was right I almost did, but the look in his eyes help he see after seeing the heart in his eyes. Once I get back to work everybody was looking at me like I was a ghost it was really quiet for a minute I'm to find out everybody that was a regular that went there, look at me said April 1st you were in a roll round attacked, April 3rd you wake up out of Acoma and now back to work not two weeks after and with not even healed all the way. He also told me that it seems like it was one of the saddest day at centerfolds that I had a lot of people crying and praying for me when I was in the hospital that DJ made everybody pray for me.

When I did appear in court. The officer didn't show but before my 4'0 breathe a lazier text and cocaine blood level was so high I thought I was going to do some Jail time. But instead the judge and had a heart to heart. She started off with do I know how lucky I'm, that god gave me another chance at life and you walked away with just stiches and a closed head injurie. She had pictures from the actuated and the numbers from the doctor of my blood level drug count and from the police officer of the breath lazier and told me a loan a 4'0 from drinking I should have been died and my heart should been out my chest from the cocaine you should of been Died twice before you left the bar, and now the officer didn't show up so she has to dismiss my case. That do I know how lucky I'm that I have a god watching over me. But from looking at me she said I think you are going through a good listen and she hope to never see me again. Said thank you and got out of their.

I did have some memory loss in the beginning car accident my kids said that I look like I didn't even know who they were at one point. My first husband start a fighting a lot. We had got into one fight so bad my first son came in the room to see a gun in my face. At one point you had me so convinced that he had rights over the kids. I tried to leave no access to getting my monies out of our accounts the earliest had to be at work open the clothing at times 7 days a week. Started to do drugs really bad so you're back and get out of the streets and bike clubs and drug dealers. Sometimes drug dealers are coming to get me to help him collect their money at times. I started to being that person you didn't mess with. I wasn't a bully. Very much respect then and what I thought was love. Is now starting seeing things and have that women in tu 'wishing started kicking in. Started to feel like anther women was in my home and some wrong was going on in my house especially in my room and the fourth floor. But when I would try and talk to husband (1) on how I was feeling. I even felt a lot of fear in my own home. I crazy maybe I need to be put on medicine. Well for a moment I was and on this medic ion start feeling even more crazy thoughts. We started fighting even to the point my first born walk in with him on top of me with a gun in my face. My drinking and doing cocaine and black outs were starting.

A year later on my birthday April 12 Drinking, cocaine it up, smoking and woke up hand cuff to a bed in the mental ward. Waking you to someone wanting to take my blood purser and asking my nurse were I'm I. She told me I was at the hospital in the mental word unit. She said at my job they revive me on stage I was dead for 3 minutes and my husband sign me in to this floor. In my mind I'm like what the Hell. Happy birthday to me. Once they got done checking me out to make sure I was okay and strictly hands is able to take a shower and you can phone come on I called my husband asking him what the hell is going on why did you knock me up in here he said because of wind drinking drums trying to kill myself. Thinking about him or the kid and all the things that we lose. I work 7 days a week at around 5,000 week. I start to get my thoughts together. Well when it came time to see the therapist she had told me make her concern was my drug level was high of cocaine but then ask me how I did I do heroin and why did I have rat poisoning and look like a household product in my system. I told her and don't do heroin and I did not try to kill myself but according to my husband last year with the accident by alcohol and cocaine level with high as well. So I had to go through the spots with her to be able to go home. And but the next day had to go back to work because I miss a lot of work already. Well here we go back to work. Was doing good for a moment but when I was coming back home started to feel there was fear inside my home again and started to find women's things that weren't mine. But got told I can't remember shit that it's probably mine. Then my stuff start to end up missing but I'm just crazy. At some point through all this tried to level with the kids but he did have rights over them because he adopted them so I was told I couldn't leave the house with them.

Started back working seven days a week opening to closing six go those days. Drinking was dam near every day and the white powered was my vitamin. Hang out and being around the club houses again. Sometimes not even showing up for days getting high all the time and drinking started not to see a way out of this light. Tell one day getting a phone call from his girlfriend calling me his wife to let me known how she in my house all the time at work even left the house why I was in it. I started to think how I was going to leave him with even my kids. Well one day when the kids went to school and he went to work. Start packing all of are close and all my jewel and some pictures and the forty five he had in my face at one time. Went up to the school and had just got out my three I was so Hart broken I had to leave my step son behind because I had no rights of him. Well I was head to a friend from my house that was from a club witch I new he wouldn't come around me because I was with them. But not to fair after I get A phone call from my 1st husband London please come back home I kept hanging up on him, when he was home he seen I went into the place where he kept the gun. He called the police and told he I stool me gun and took are kids out of school. I told the cop I had got rid of the gun and the kids were fine we are going to safety with them because I'm done with being abused. He ask why I didn't call the police on him and I told him I did and you officers told me don't get into domestics valence. And I told him to please stop calling and I hung up, started to go up to where I needed to be safe and my new family. Back to club family

Time for a Storm to Ride

Well good thing is me, kids and ma and brother moved back in together in New Baltimore to get us out of the city area off the water. Had a Roommate every now and then would help out the dancers to get on their feet or ones trying to move in from out of town. Started dating again went back hanging out with the bike clubs again.

Things started getting crazy again still working as a dancer and one day came to the guys house I was dating he left for a moment and a women showed up, to let me know that her old man and mine were at these girls house. She took me there and seen him kissing this girl though the front window. So I through A rock though it when they looked made sure they seen my face. We try and work it out but he cheated on me again. One of his club bother take me to the hospital because I try to punch the window out.

This started to get more out of hand drugs were daily and drinking my ma always took care of the kids why I took care of her and my brother. I started waking up hanging out off of Woodwardd downtown different clubs and different places on the street losing control ex-husband trying to get me back. So one day one of the dancers I got along with also worked out in Las Vegas she ask me a couple of times before I went. By the third visit I did meet someone and went out with him, we were drinking and he had some weed and what I thought was coke cane. He put some in one of the joints. I found out later it was meth and it was going up my nose. Well that was a onetime deal. I woke up next to him married. Don't remember where or when that night but my last time. Moved my ma, brother and kids out with me. My ma woke to a moving truck in front of the house and told my ma and brother pack it up and see you in couple of days and divorced him in the meantime. Started working more at Sphere entertainment. The Bars out here were open24/7.

If you were new you started the shift they told or they needed to and the better you did your job you went to a better shift. Love how the girls put on shows and you had to as well or didn't work their or you had a shift. One afternoon I was asked to work. I see these few guys walk in and found out they were from New Jersey. Well didn't realize I was meeting my second husband. We had a great Time while he was there. We gave each other numbers and me and my brother drop him and his friends off it was crazy we both started to cry.

Well not to long after I went to go visit him in New Jersey. Well back in Vegas started to have a problem with the guy I first meet their. Rocks through my widows and wouldn't leave us alone. And Jersey and I wanted to be with each anther but if I move there I couldn't dance anymore. Well gave my Ma and brother five a piece and the kids were still talking to my first still and until I got my act together trying to see what I would do out there for a living. Only James and Jackie stayed with their adopted dad at the time, LA came with me but visit them at times Started working at shopper market was a self-shopper and did army base order they had in anther apartment in the store they had started after 911. I so Love that place and so miss all the people there. Before I know it I'm going to be having a baby are Bell to be. The people at my job were a family to me. Deb was my best friend love her. Had a beautiful Jersey baby shower. We were building on a bigger place so we can get James and Jackie back here. We always gave my ma bus tickets for them to come and see us. Well the last time my ma and the kids went back a week later I have police call me from Michigan. They had my kids and that one was getting beating and one was being rape with a bunch of anther little girls in the house. Well I had got on the first bus back there and almost through being pregnant I went back fighting and trying not lose my mind or kill someone. His girlfriend at the time he has her looking like my twin. Come to find out she was using my identity right down to my social security number. I had one out burst out in court, I had to stop because I was also present. To sit in that court room listening to what he did to all these little girls and boys and had two girl- friend's there too and knew what was going on and I'm sitting by them. God was there that day. Things that were going through mind. Not only I was going to get my two baby's back from the state they were watching over because I had LA and a baby to be and making sure husband too was on the up and up. He was a firemen volunteer and he told me stories about 911 and he was a manager for a copier company as well. After I had Bell in New Jersey the child welfare from Detroit had got a hold of child welfare their and her dad and grand- parents were there as well and they had no reason they were going to take her that we were going back to Detroit Michigan to get my two babies back. I so bad didn't want to leave New Jersey was so happy their and still to this day I miss my Jersey family so much. I went through two years off fight to get them back because of whatever They told me I had to do I did and then they were trying to tell me that after two years whatever person they were placed with could or have the chance to adopt them. Said there will be no way in hell that I'm alive and did everything and more to get my kids back they were going tell this bull. Well we had not even two weeks to get back to Detroit.

A good friend of mine that helped find houses Jersey put money down on the house to buy it and we made a good home and the state finely left us alone. Well once we became settled and a family.

Jersey paid for our wedding here. Two fear after that the twins were going to be born. Well between all this I had to stay in bed a lot when I was parent with them and had to even stop them from coming to earlier. A little w bit later after I had them found out Husband too cheated with someone very close that they had sex on the bar of our home in the basement why I'm across the street and when I was laid up in bed, he was messing around with someone at the bar. Well after finding this all out I went to the bar finely came home. Things would never be the same as much as I wanted things to be fix the trust was broken.

Started back at the dance clubs here drinking, drugs and stay out not coming home tell the day. I didn't know how to stop and turn back to let things be fixed but him knowing what we went through and how I was played and hurt by my first husband can't fix it. The real hardest thing I had to do was leave all my kids their and walkaway. But once I got a place, he would let me see them again. When I wasn't working in the dance clubs, or getting girls together and making money from them. I even opened up my own Dominatricks office Dungan.

Where we did seasons and webcamming and even putting our shows together. The women of the night and darkness. Through all this my mother had died from sorrows of the liver April 10 two days before my birthday when Bell was 3 months old. She never got to see the twins. I started to lose a lot of my heart it was going cold and dark and hate. Had even got another divorce. Didn't fight him for the girl not that I didn't want them, it was the life I was starting to live again and didn't want to make a second mistake by getting them hurt by someone I might be with. I went from being the girl you go to when you wanted have and was in a different clubs or somewhere on the streets or bartending to dancing and doing dominatrick sessions every night, seven days a week. I started wanting to have someone to really love me be their ride to die. Not a show or who could get and cheating on me. But the things I was doing I was the madam or just a fun piece of meat to be around. But I did have a few of clubs that did make me feel like family and was there for me when need. My Little brother Rick was starting to go through some crazy things himself. He was trying to keep it together with his job and church. But his mental health, gambling and being a lone until he got a hold of a hooker he would see off and on and started to get high with her again. He came into some money again. I had got a phone call on a Saturday walking into work from aunt that my brother was dead and because I'm his sister I had to go make sure that it was his body. Well they called it as an over dose with heron. His face was black and blue he didn't look right and talking to his pastor my brother had four thousand on him Friday. But no money was found. I even had his phone I had his hooker at one point thinking i was him texting her, like he was still alive even almost met her at his apartment I had friends talk me out of it. That was really hard at that point I was cold and felt I had no family anymore witch everybody was dyeing around me. My first son LA was in the middle of boot camp in the Army. My brother was their when he had got sworn in. I had a friend that was doing some building work out in DC.

I knew him for long time he even took a flight to be there for me at my brother's funeral. I was talk to him on the phone, packed up my stuff even had my ma and brothers ashes in there vases in the front seat and drove all the way there. Had to get away but realize I had to go back because I still had my kids there. Went back drinking and doing drugs taking girls to party's to make money and doing Dom sessions working to make sure everybody had what they needed.

Well one day coming from a Monday night football party that I was called on with some girls, I didn't make it home. I had police pull me over. The one time I didn't drink or get high. They check my car looked in my trunk witch had a lot of support stuff trying to ask me crazy questions about it and I played dumb and asked them why they pulled me over. Well they did find a tazer and two loose pills in my purse, later at the jail they found pot also. Had to get a lawyer quick but couldn't call anyone to come get me because they had my phones. I was missing to everybody I knew for three days. Friends of mine said they went to the office hoping they didn't find my body. Well someone finely found me. I had got a lawyer and they want to give eleven year wipins and drugs charges. I did two years pro bastion and doing drug tests for almost a year. I moved in with Pops that I met at the bartending I was at Bears and a couple days a week dancing and had to close down my office, I had my office Dungeon because I had bills, kids and payments to the lawyer and whatever else the courts had me pay. Well One day someone that was my teen age crush back when I was sixteen came in and was in a middle of joining a club. Well we started to see each other. I almost couldn't believe we were together being with your teenage crush, becoming his patch old ladies'. Had such beautiful times together. Loved that I was a part of a family, had help or put holidays together, for the brothers and sisters and kids. Fun ridding tripe's good and beautiful sister hood. But after a while things started to get crazy to a point. We were beating on each other until we were bleeding or someone was early hurt. The last fight I had gotten into with him I took a brass lamb to my face. I know he need help he was in a bad mental state of mind and a loss of a child can put someone over the edge. Trying to be there for him about two years and thinking I can help him had to stop. I was not making things better or he didn't want me to. My heart was crushed I was so hurt. But couldn't stick around to help him because the way things were looking one of us would of end up dead or both. The one thing I did really, hate the most I just didn't lose him I lost a family as well and was one club that really just made me a family and a sister.

I was never the Madame to them or the go to girl. I was proud to be the patch, And also lost my home family life and thank you for those sister that are still sisters. I even lost my normal job working home care. Well one day he was going out of town and I packed up my stuff. I always prayed for him to find peace with his self and will always care and always love and I did forgive him for what he has done to me a crazy kind of love for each other, just hope he can be happy. Moved to nine mile area. Had at first mama pearl and my sissy were a lot of support and always no matter what or who I was with they were always family to me. I kept praying for help or sending me a sine or someone I didn't want to go back to doing things I didn't want to. I had got back InTouch with some people from another club or they weren't in clubs no more. I know a lot of people were upset what he had done to me. I started hanging out with my best friend Georgie and this guy that was over there didn't realize at first who he was because of how upset I was at the time and mentally putting myself back together. His club was the only club that put my picture up when one of their brothers that I was real close as brother and sister we had got close after my brother passed. But had to remind me who he was because he cut his hair off and long bread off and I knew him as Rez. It took a couple of times I was almost scared to go on a date with him but why not look at what I have been through already. I was so hurt inside and so broken I couldn't feel myself again and so I didn't want to go through again, everything I have been through. He showed me a different way of life.

Well you would think one nice dinner turn into such a beautiful life changing moment. Mentally, Physically and very much spiritually. My first moment meeting his family, the most that I love about his family you can see there was closeness and been through family life things even with natural parents not being together but trying to keep it together as a family and being their at family gatherings. Thank you my Mother In-law's and Father In-Iaws for everything. I love you so much and His grandparents, so old fashioned with some values warms my heart. To my sister in- laws and Brother In-laws also have a lot love for you guys.

At the time and moments I have been through I would never change it. I do forgive the all wrong of hand that have been on me and hope you have found God in your life at one point. To my kids fathers I do thank you for are beautiful kids and I hope you grow and learned from you mistakes and have better life's and relationships. Especial Love sent out to a couple of the brothers for still being always there. Love you guys. And my dearest Dolin thank you for answering my prayers from God and showing me there is real love, Loyalty, friendship and fight for what we believe in. I know I am A handful and crazy at times but we have a lot of laugher and we keep each anther on are toes. To my step son love that you are in my life, let's try and stay close as a family and looking forward to see the future as a family brings. To my first three born child, love you guys with all my heart I know we have been through hell and back and there is nothing guys I wouldn't do for you. I feel that what we went through made us stronger and know how to fight for each other even as a family. I know I'm not your normal ma. But hope I have showed you how to served life and never judge and keep an open mind with everybody and never let your grad down. But if you do never stand down, each time you fall you came up each time stronger. I am glade you are making yourself better then what I have done. Tells me I did do my job right. All the hurt. scarps and bruises I feel no more my worries. My LA and my Jamie James and my Jack Attack. Keep making things better in your life and stronger you got this Hope is real guys. To my three monkeys. Thank you for loving me so unconditionally. Thank you for showing me how to be a kid. And going to learn about teen hood and being a girl or young lady. But just remember their whole army behind you loves. You guys have a lot to learn and please lesson.

Closing Thoughts

1. Innocents; When it is taken away from you without a choice. Not knowing a real childhood with being in fear.
2. Deception; Seeing all the lawyer for what it was Worth. Someone showing you a good life to find out nothing but lies.
3. Deceit; What you see is not always real.
4. Death; feeling yourself out of body's and watching your heart grow cold from hurt from your love ones leaving.
5. Alcoholism and Drugs; Doin both, dealing with family members and dealing them myself.
6. Being in the sex industry; self my self and making a business out of it.
7. Gambling; my brother to the point your are harming your family sister and kids.
8. Marriage; know bad ones and finely finding the really things that devoice really had come with it.
9. Identity; Some that looks like and is being you to the fullest.
10. Mental and Physical; 40 years off and on
11. Money; the price you pay for [Me and my brother]
12. Finding out when your kids are hart
13. Past teenage crush
14. Army ma
15. Happy ever after?

With this storm ride of life, no matter what go through. You get up you find that help. Do not live by (well this is how I was raise,) Bull I always teach my kids you be better than your father and I. Your kids should one more above to keep braking changes of the past and make a difference.

Are past doesn't live us. We change it and keep God close to you on life, he really gets you through it. Change your circle of friends you have to. Keep going forward, the darkness will wear away and the light will get brighter. This next section I shared some photos some letters and poem's of my life.

Well you would think one nice dinner turn into such a beautiful life changing moment. Mentally, Physically and very much spiritually. My first moment meeting his family, the most that I love about his family you can see there was closeness and been through family life things even with natural parents not being together but trying to keep it together as a family and being their at family gatherings. Thank you my Mother In-law`s and Father In-Iaw`s for everything. I love you so much and His grandparents, so old fashioned with some values warms my heart. To my sister in-laws and Brother In-laws also have a lot love for you guys.

To mama thank you for being here no matter what and loving me like one of your own. To my sissy I have never had a sister like you and would never change it for the world. To my long life friend, we go back over twenty years and we never missed a beat with whatever is going on. Always pray for to win your fight with Cancer. To a long life friends out there you who you are thank you for being around. To my mama you have been in my life almost 30 years, you were out for a minute but slide right back in place. To those sisters that never left my side love you forever. To my Driver Ride to Die can't wait to tell that story. Love you so.

To Dad you might not be blood but it doesn't take that to be a father. To my Church Family I love you all so dearly I would need to write a book about you guys, thank for never letting me go. I was Baptized at my Church by my Pastor thank you for not x me out because I wanted to take you under with me. But felt a lot of love that day, even had a Baptism buddy Pat, love her so and forever in my happy place. At the time and moments I have been through I would never change it. I do forgive the all wrong of hand that have been on me and hope you have found God in your life at one point. To my kids fathers I do thank you for are beautiful kids and I hope you grow and learned from you mistakes and have better lives and relationships.

Especial Love sent out to a couple of the brothers for still being always there. Love you guys. And my dearest Dolin thank you for answering my prayers from God and showing me there is real love, Loyalty, friendship and fight for what we believe in. I know I am A handful and crazy at times but we have a lot of laugher and we keep each anther on are toes. To my step son love that you are in my life, let's try and stay close as a family and looking forward to see the future as a family brings.

To my first three born child, love you guys with all my heart I know we have been through hell and back and there is nothing guys I wouldn't do for you. I feel that what we went through made us stronger and know how to fight for each other even as a family. I know I'm not your normal ma. But hope I have showed you how to served life and never judge and keep a open mind with everybody and never let your grad down. But if you do never stand down, each time you fall you came up each time stronger. I am glad you are making yourself better then what I have done. Tells me I did do my job right. All the hurt. Scars and bruises I feel no more my worries. My LA and my Jamie James and my Jack Attack. Keep making things better in your life and stronger you got this

Hope is real guys.

To my three monkeys. Thank you for loving me so unconditionally. Thank you for showing me how to be a kid. And going to learn about teen hood and being a girl or young lady. But just remember their whole army behind you loves. You guys have a lot to learn and please lesson.

Comments

(DAD)

You've become more then just a random dancer you wild at first but not stupid. You took one day at a time grew in college and in heart you have that drive to be better. You've became more of a family member than just a friend I've seen you grow mind and spirit I'm glade and proud to call you daughter I would give my last breath to keep you alive if needed I truly love you and the person you've become just writing this is making me cry like I'm writing a eulogy when someone dies but you've been reborn in every way since. Since I'm out of words and can't spell words worth crap' I leave you with this, the world would be a empty place with you and your love.